CATBIRD

Catbird

©Julia Marie Davis, 2024

Books may be purchased in quantity and/or special sales by contacting the publisher. All inquiries related to such matters should be addressed to:

Middle Creek Publishing & Audio
9161 Pueblo Mountain Park Road
Beulah, CO 81023
editor@middlecreekpublishing.com
(719) 369-9050

First Paperback Edition, 2024
ISBN: 978-1-957483-23-8
Cover Art: DALL-E AI Image generated but edited and altered.
Cover Design: David Anthony Martin, Middle Creek Publishing & Audio
Author Image:

CATBIRD

JULIA MARIE DAVIS

Middle Creek Publishing & Audio
Beulah, CO   USA

Written in the weeks after the invasion of Ukraine, Feb 24, 2022, with recent revisions and additions in 2024

 February 25, 2022

An earthworm. I pick it up in a gloved hand. It wriggles in my grasp. The worm reminds me of fishing, putting worms on hooks, my brothers chopping them in half, waiting until each end wriggles away. One of our favorite childhood pastimes. I gently lay it on the ground.

The skies are bright, yet I feel shrapnel falling.

In my dreams, missiles haunt the early morning hours of my awakening. A sheering of metal, rubble-covered corpses, some with heads and some not, some facing down and others faceting, litter my dreams and haunt my thoughts.

I kneel to tend my garden. A meow-like bird call distracts me. The grey Catbird is singing. I watch it flit to the top of a branch and glance up at the cumulous heavens—the ones I watched as I lay in the backyard in childhood, tracing bunnies in the clouds.

Yet today, when I look up, I shudder. I rub my eyes and wipe a crunch of sand away.

I wait and wonder. Will it grow dark? Will we hear the thunder first?

Inside my mind is smoke. Is dark. Is noise.

Clouds that come to get us in the night.

In the morning, before we might wake to rubble all around us.

My bright, clear sky is free of bombs, free of debris, free of screaming children fleeing while their parents lay dying in their beds. This sky is clear, guiltily clear.

My heart is heavy with the news of this morning. This is only the beginning, they say.

ii.   March 1, 2022

The fruits of victory are not tumbling quickly into the mouth of the aggressor. I think about Winston Churchill – We shall never surrender – he said. I try to shake off my sense of fear.

The sun is out, and it is warm, and it is morning and I greet the grey Catbird at my feet. He has come for my husband, who left for the city at dawn. The bird hops and pecks, near but not too close, as I snip dead roses to make way for new buds. This is my morning routine of late. Gardening and sitting on the porch sipping coffee gets me out of the house, away from the television set and the news. And the dark.

The sky looms this morning with clouds, with coming rain. Predicted, anyway, as the weather never turns out as they say it will, much like this war. The news I hear this morning is disturbing to process. My heart is in a panic, and I look at the sky. I have the sense of bombs falling. Though the sky seems clear. We are near a major city, my husband and I whisper to each other in the hours before dawn as we try to sleep, as this nightmare is about to begin. If they drop a nuke here, we are dead. We know it, yet we pretend not to know. We say it then gently tiptoe around reality, joking that we will head for the Adirondacks and the old shack I inherited if we need to pretend it's a viable plan. We are essentially in the biggest metropolis in the world though technically we are ten miles away; we know it and we ignore it. We have to pretend. It is the trade-off of living near a city like this one or anywhere just outside its borders.

In these times I think of my parents, growing up during the Second World War, losing uncles neighbors fathers even cousins in Europe last heard of dying somewhere running in a forest taking cover in a building, hiding under a desk. I think of my father listening on his handheld radio, hearing news of France being taken, of London being bombed, of Pearl Harbor under siege, and I think of him saying goodbye to his uncle, nine years older and 18 when he became a marine. I think of my father's father, standing guard on the front lines of three wars including the First World War, knowing what he'd seen heard done and didn't do that shaped his stolid grim presence. Things he never spoke about. What lay behind the jokes, the grin. What his hands his bullets must have done. Zeus, they called him. So, you know. Death.

I think of my mother, her sister, and grandmother waving goodbye to my thirty-eight-year-old Papa. I think about the letters he sent my grandmother, the love poems, the loneliness in the line: I don't hear much from you people. And what that might mean. My grandfather in France near the end of the war, writing on the back of the brochure of a French Cathedral. There is love in this, even when I find a small slip of paper forty years later in Papa's desk in lovely handwriting and an address in the Czechoslovakia.

Pearl Harbor. The bombing that got us into World War II. I think what will get us into this thing — this World War III. I say it and everyone shakes their head at me. But I wonder what my mother my father their parents heard on the radio that evening. What they did. Where they went. What they ate. Did they get an ice cream? Did they walk to school? Did my small boy of a father do his paper route that day? Did they cry? I feel smidges of blood and smoke seeping into their brains their minds watching reels at movie theatres. A silent scream.

On the day of Pearl Harbor, my mother's parents knew, I am sure, that the three years spent traveling and training officers around the country would end with Papa leaving for Europe. Or did they suppose as a reservist and as a man of almost 40 he'd be spared? A man who came to this country to be a citizen then to fight for freedom against Nazis to watch friends die to shoot to bring home German guns and a sword and medals and a horn.

All that emptying out into the blood that is mine.

Did my grandfather have time to pack my mother and her sister and her mother up and move with them to my aunt's farm? Or had my grandmother done that on her own?
12

iii.   March 4, 2022

Are we fighting to enslave or are we fighting to make room for honesty to live? To make room for fairness? For integrity? For what is right? I come out to my safe porch, nine feet wide, a porch swing, a perfect haven and I wonder when it will happen here. We are near the largest metropolis in the country, and at this writing, I am too afraid to write this, really.

It is early March, yet the buds of a warm spring push their way through.

I argue over text with friends who say – politicians do nothing but sit around and have lunches with donors and smile for the cameras. This is a familiar rant set up in their minds by media groups online. They cannot fathom the strings of troll farms copywriters leaded hands typing theories into laptops, creating taglines to incite. I try to remind them that these so-called politicians who smile for the camera awaken well before dawn, deal with classified and war-related and terrorism-related and espionage-related information each morning.

And maybe go to sleep by midnight on lucky days. And know things far worse than we do.

My friends know what kind of work I have done, and they cannot argue with me.

We get it, they tell me. Just wanting me to shut up and not to tell truths.

Just to slam it into them, I remind them that these people work until they drop trying to do their best for our country. Even the ones they do not like.

It's so obvious, I say, what these dictators want to do.

The plan is to install a puppet government.

The plan isn't working, and the people are fighting like no one expected.

Like the Militia fought to form America.

Putin expected them to hand themselves over to him.

To slink off like the Afghans did.

I'm not looking for a lift, I am looking for an ally, President Zelensky said.

To the world's surprise.

Who would hand over their land to a thug?

Who would give a murderer, a KGB man, their country? No one.

Unless they are puppets themselves.

Unless they have been propped up with loans and gifts and purchases of houses for twice the asking price. Propped up by greed and that sliver of sociopath inside of them. (Twenty-five percent of all people are sociopaths. Believe it or not.)

This is World War Three, I say back in text and three dots linger, then they go on to their coffee and their work shaking their heads as if I have gone mad. But I know I have not.

The Catbird flits up the porch steps. Sam calls out to it from inside the screen door, and it hop hops toward him.

iv.   March 6, 2022

Silt filters past in my eyes, concrete crumbles in my dreams of falling beams, of human wreckage. My heart is beating fast, and I am running. Running from someone. I open my eyes. Sunlight filters into my bedroom. I am lying face down and my lovely husband is in the bathroom. Half-awake. I am still half-dreaming of bombs of shelters of mothers and babies, of old women getting on buses. Of young men dying. I close the door, telling him I don't want to hear his noises, that I want to sleep some more. I lie between wake and sleep in a cocoon of white sheets and puffy comforter, warm, safe, until the creaking of the floors gets to me as my husband paces around getting dressed and I think, hoping to awaken me. He slips under the sheets, warming his hands on my naked skin, pulls me to him. To make guilty love in the early morning light. I am guilty. I am guilty. I am. Guilty. I feel that we are all guilty. For what?

I hear his CBS morning news radio program as I am dressing. He listens as he is shaving.

A baby raped. Children locked in basements, girls tortured, men with fingers, limbs chopped off by whom – soldiers who claim they didn't want any part of this war,

Crammed into spaces so they can only stand, cannot sleep.

I cannot bear it.

I go downstairs to make coffee.

My stomach turns as I think of the mothers, the sons, the daughters, the baby.

Why is rape still the work of war?

Why is it something the news still wants to hide?

We hear of it only once, maybe twice. But we know what's happening.

Zelensky repeats his call - I need weapons, not an escape ride.

v.   March 9, 2022

It is a Wednesday, and I sit on the porch drinking coffee my mind pacing back and forth in the streaming morning light. In an unfair world where I am safe. Pink with white, a delicate circle of Rosebuds frame the edges of the rail. Rhododendrons, spring mauve clumps, bursting daffodils, and tulip buds peek out through fresh cedar mulch, and hyacinths lavendering pads an early siren of spring.

I can't help but read the news. It's a compulsion that I do try to control. A murderous dictator ramming T-62s model 1967 and young men of his own into a war they've not been taught to fight, cramming boys spawned on video games and television and tech jobs and goatees and scruffy beards and globalism and light-RTV, weaning them from their mothers' worlds with promises is hard to look away from. The newscasters say the US Government believes this skirmish will end within weeks. That Putin is overconfident, unrealistic.

I think of Thomas Paine's "these are the times that try men's souls." I think of "tyranny, like hell, is not easily conquered." My heart is racing, and it is not yet 8 o'clock in the morning.

I now say that this war is intentional, that Putin will not leave this war until he is in a coffin. He is in this to either win it or die. Again, my husband thinks I read the news too much. The news is my business, I tell him. I know, I know. My work in intelligence and now as a crisis expert pays enough for me to steal away some of my time to write. I fell into it, really, and I got good at it, at reading the news, analyzing trends, writing speeches and statements. Sometimes lining up a wall of armed guards and making statements on camera. I surprise myself at how poised I seem on television. That person seems disconnected from the me I live with at home. The one who writes and photographs obsessively in between answering calls and emails and making statements and analyzing situations and doing crisis plans to earn money.

I am mistrustful this morning.

I do not believe people's intentions now. I see the conspiracy of the conspiracies; I predict each move that certain unnamed politicians make. I've had to respond to some of this coddled right-winger's statements, their purposeful anti-anti-dis-establishmentarianism.

Every person walking by has bushy eyebrows this morning, pudgy bodies, looking down and away, too busy to wave. Walking highly groomed, well-behaved dogs. My husband goes in to refresh his coffee. One man's dog stops to pee on the line of grass between the sidewalk and the street. Rabbits hop madly under the porch as the Airedale makes his mark. A Robin flies past the dog's uplifted leg. A black SUV screeches past, bypassing the main road. The man is looking at his phone: dark hair, mottled skin. I cannot make out his eyes.

It is only 7:50 am but we've already had a lifetime of day. I've read the news. I've edited and sent out a press release. I've thought deeply about the wounds these people get, about the drunken soldiers wearing women's fur coats out of their houses after plundering them inside and outside of their bodies, as they carry out all the food they can find. As Putin stops the grain deal from moving along. As he bombs bridges because it is Putin and his supporters, his puppets, his men around the world and in his country. Men of men who want the white of white to stay white and to put women back into their place with the controlled.

The grey Catbird flits two feet away; he waits for my husband to come out. A ray of sunlight hits the porch where I sit, soaking up the warmth. A crumpled dixie cup squished under the railing. A pile of acorns, stripped by foraging squirrels, lies under the porch swing. The bird hop hops. Meew Meews. I sit quiet, trying to find something uplifting in the Times. Watching him peck. Peck. Peck. Waiting. Waiting. Lading. Lading. Meeew. Meeew. Chirp. Meeew. What do you want from me, bird, I say softly under my breath. He hops one step farther from me.

My feathered visitor moves to the blue plate I've taken to spreading with jelly and placing on the steps each morning, the one my mother gave me from her Polish mother who married my Ukrainian grandfather, the 38-year-old reservist officer training expert who went to fight for freedom and this country and righteousness and democracy and against genocide and hatred and not this. Genocide. Hatred. Everywhere. You will be next, I keep thinking. They are coming for your books first, then your bodies, then everything else. I hear what sounds like a brown hawk call and look for the one who visits our climbing tree in the front yard, but in the branch above, I see a Blue Jay. Flapping, squawking. The mimic. He flies low past the porch and the Catbird hops close to the front door.

Every man walking by now to catch the train or the bus to the city reminds me of my Ukrainian grandfather, my mother's father. Close-cropped dark blond hair, thinning and lashed neatly across his square head, a wide friendly smile, grey-blue eyes, stocky, muscular build. A walk like my husband's that says, I'll kill you if you get too close to me, but don't make me do it. My husband learned that walk in Pittsburgh, growing up in the 60s, just as the steel mills shut down. The "Still Mills." When the air was black, and the creeks ran brown.

Thick skies deep with ash covered the city. Back when the war between the lord merchant oligarch mine owner and the sycophant worker hadn't entirely undone itself if it ever has or ever will. Or is this what this war is all about. Who's on top, as they say.

Another man walks past, looking at the slate sidewalk with intent.

Am I surrounded by spies? I think: Is it that kind of day?

We all feel on edge maybe, living so close to the biggest city in the country – perhaps nearly one of the biggest in the world - that in reality could be bombed. That was bombed in 2001 in fact, daily reminders as we see the air space where the twin towers once stood lit up several times a month. Brothers killing brothers, I think, this is terrorism too.

Buzzing in our eyes and a ringing in our ears remind us of our vulnerability.

A pit in our stomachs as we walk under safe skies.

We must move away from here soon.

The Catbird hop-hops and cheeps when my husband - tall, big-shouldered, gentle Sam – appears with his coffee in hand, his coumadin and a banana, the daily reminder between him and his demise, what might have been his destiny in a blood clot twenty years before. I like to tell him and myself God saved him so that I could get to him finally. Get to safety at last. Get to a point where I wasn't dating questioning divorcing singling lonelying haggering ageing like a frightened goose flapping off to the horizon.

The bird lurches toward him. My husband looks at him approvingly. Hello, little bird, he says. You're still here, are you? As if the bird is going to disappear, I think, frustrated at his fatalism when it comes to nature. The Catbird follows him slightly, and I move the dish under the porch swing where he pecks at the preserves in the dish. How do you know it's a he? I ask my husband. I see his ladybird sitting on the nest when I go out into the backyard to stretch before you wake up, Sam answers. Oh, my husband loves to eat and drink, clearly. But he is one to exercise as well, and I hope that this means that the blood clot will never return as long as he takes his medicine, which is why he has his banana in the morning to buffer the morning pills and keep the potassium high. Are you my ladybird? Sam says as he leans in to kiss me. We read the Times. I try to stay off my phone and read about new books, about art, about photography, about new restaurants opening.

vi.   March 10, 2022

Murder is in the air and we are 7,500 miles from Kiev. The Catbird hops a bit closer, chirps, meews, chirps, pecks a route away from us. Then a hop circle near him. The news selectively reports murders every few days or every week, but assaults happen daily. Why do they not publish the horror, the rapes, the murder that happens on the insides of war? My husband shakes his head and doesn't want to hear more of the horrors. I hear it on the radio in the mornings, I know, he always says. His father's childhood was enough to hear about, he says, growing up and out of the coal mining villages that took the labor and siphoned the life out of the workers. Battles with soot and ash. Battles with hunger. And then his father himself escaping the Battle of the Bulge and certain death with the luck of trench foot that eventually brought him home.

As Sam stands, the bird hops from the dish, mewing and cheeping. This bird is watching my husband, following him as he steps toward the chair.

Catbird, he says, Good morning.

The bird stands in front of him, toe to toe. They stare at one other, and the Catbird cocks his head. What? my husband whispers though he is not a whisperer.

Eventually my husband walks inside with his coffee to go upstairs to work.

I watch him in his Levi jeans. The bird watches him go, hides behind a plant.

And then the Catbird bird pecks his way down steps under bushes and away from me.

I am of no use to him this twitty little man-bird who doesn't have the time of day for me. A serious business kind of flyer, intent, intent. I am not part of his intent.

vii.   March 12, 2022

Rat-a-tat-tat of machine guns ring in my ears and I shut off the morning news to sit on the porch, to check the weather, to soak in the early morning sun. I open the news app on my phone but try to limit myself to five minutes. Saturday morning. My husband is sleeping in.

According to a recent census, Russian is the native language of 29% of Ukrainians. Some of these people were bussed out of the area before the war, now barely being fed inside the invading country. My grandmother's parents were from Lomza, Poland, part of Russia in the 1880s, a crossroads, a multi-cultural place where various cultures and religions lived among one another. Why did they leave in 1900? I don't know. In 1944, the town was wiped out.

I know nothing of the Ukrainian past of my grandfather. I can feel the blood flow. That is all.

At the beginning of the war, the news chattered away about the sympathizers at the border. How many of them were packed up by Russia, taken from their homes and sent in busses to the mother country? As if they'd really asked for this.

No one talks about them now. The last thing we heard was they were given $120 in Russian money for food each week (or month) and housed somewhere.

Are they dead or alive? No one would know. They are inside. Banished to God-knows.

They are the ones, news reports say, who wanted to be part of Russia. As if they are to blame for this and not the social media propaganda run by Putin trolls.

I wonder what they think these months later as their houses are flattened by tanks, their land burned, ransacked. As they hear about crops and neighbors and relatives tortured, dying. As they watch their villages and towns fall to ash. Does it become personal, then?

An ad for light cotton sweaters floats across my phone screen, enticing me to click on Summer Linens. I am feckless—shopping online for white clothing, looking at lovely, quite clean-looking new dresses that I do not need—that I will later buy on sale for no occasion.

I am guilty of something.

Before my grandfather left to fight in World War II, he moved with my mother and her sister, and my grandmother moved every three months during the early days of the war. Training officers, my grandfather was a reservist who'd been called up, a thirty-eight-year-old Corporal., turned Lieutenant Colonel.

I think of my mother now, making friends at ten years old, reinventing a new self every time she moved. An improved self, she told me later. Adapting a new accent. Feigning a new laugh. A new persona. Living in a motel cottage smaller than my bedroom. My mother hasn't forgotten this skill and sometimes I catch her being someone else, the memory seared into her cells. Her people, she says, were killed in the Holocaust. Not just Jews. Random Poles slaughtered just for helping, for being sympathetic, for hiding friends and neighbors…and five million Ukranian Jews.

Someone with my mother's genes is going to die today, is all I can think.

I look up at the pale sky, clouds float by and I can hear the surprise and the horror and the shells and see the bodies. I can feel their breath seeping out and trying to hold onto the air.

I see darkness in a lightened sky and wonder – when will it strike?

Are we next?

28

viii.　March 14, 2022

How clever. Putin calls the Ukrainians Nazis. His soldiers claim to believe that Nazis have taken over their neighboring country. Zelensky is Jewish, so this can't be a credible excuse. But it's a claim they like to push, at least for now, this beginning of the war. *Reichskommissariat.*

When will this end? I say aloud the following week on Monday when we resume having our coffees on the porch, amidst the blooming forsythia buds and pink rose buds popping out at 7 am, the Catbird pecks and waits for my husband's appearance. He hops as if trying to get my husband to come with him somewhere.

None of our people were Nazis. I know that one thing.

Surely the mud will stop them, the news says. Surely. You wonder what kind of spring it will be with the news of tanks rolling over muddy ground. With the hope the slushy ground will deter them. With the worry that they will not. This is a mucky spring with frost melting quickly in the East. Not a good sign. The cover of the New Yorker is a black and white image of a Russian tank coming up over a mushy hillside, its tracks admitting that the mud of spring is stopping no one. Is stopping at nothing. Is without a conscience. That war is without a soul. Operation Barbarossa.

We hope though. In my head I listen for airplanes. For bombs. They are coming in the form of napalm news stories. Pretending we are not in this fight.

We hope collectively yet I take my morning walks imagining planes flying overhead. Dropping bombs. I feel them dropping in the pit of my stomach. Into my soul. Destruction of all that is new, Western, democratic, progressive. Destruction of all that is accepting, all that is equal, all this is fair, all that is in the shrapnel of demo-crazy. I can hear the ash falling.

I look up at the clear skies. US Fighter Jets must be way up there, protecting us, I have to believe. I think I hear them at night when the traffic and the trains grow silent.

They are there – my husband reassures me - you just can't see them. We are close to the ultimate target, as we well know. If it hits the city, there is nowhere to escape.

ix. March 15, 2022

Grey Catbirds prefer areas with non-coniferous trees. We have three oriental spruces in the back that we planted for the New Englander in me, so I could have evergreen in the yard. I need my Christmas trees; I told my husband seven years ago when I moved in. I need to decorate them with red lights, green lights, and the blue ones. Each tree has its own color and I pretend to leave the lights up all winter for the four children who live next door. It is March and it is time to take them down. One day after work we set ourselves up to unwind three months of growth. It is spring of 2022 and the world is still working from home, and we set up little projects every day to keep ourselves from going mad. There's where the Catbird's nest is, Sam tells me as we work, pointing to the lone pine branch that hovers just above his car.

Catbirds prefer to live in areas with little traffic, thickets where their nests will not be raided or disturbed by Blue Jays or Robins in the continual fight for territory. Occasionally, they nest in a yard, according to the Audubon manual. Why has this little one chosen to be next above my husband's car, low down, and not in the thicket of a fence or the spruces, out in the open, it would seem. I wonder about this as I look up the natural nesting sites of Catbirds that afternoon. This Catbird has set his trust in us, or at least, in my husband. I don't know why he hasn't chosen a better thicket for his nest. I don't know why he is waiting for us as we finish our work and pack my dear holiday lights into boxes. Cheep, cheep, meew, meew, he says to us. We are busy so we walk past him. Our grey friend with the square tail cocks his head.

x.   March 16, 2022

It is early morning, and we are in the backyard. My husband is pulling his car out of the garage. The Camaro he cherishes because it reminds him of the '70s. He bought it during a hard moment of his life. One we do not speak about now.

The Catbird hops on the grass where Sam parks the car, next to my husband. Meew. Meew. Flies up onto the Camaro. Then onto the branch hanging over the driveway. What are you looking for, little bird? I whisper, careful not to scare him off. He is busy hopping from car to branch.

I watch my husband come back out of the house several times, coffee in hand, with the bag of waters, granola bars, and a banana that I set out for him to eat as he makes his way through the city to the job site. It is a long day for him. He looks up into the tree as he settles his things into the car. He's dressed neatly in a light blue-button down, new Levi jeans and work boots. He looks handsome and official. His hard hat rests on the back seat.

I met you when you wore suits, I say to him, grab his shoulders, lean up to kiss him. This makes him smile. Most days, we wander around the house in our sweat-clothes, lost in emails and conference calls. You look nice, I tell him. He's busy examining the tree branch. I think what he would have been like if he hadn't been born between wars. If he had been born just a few years earlier if he had gone to Vietnam. Would he be here, even?

The Catbird has his nest in a branch that hangs over the driveway. I watch him walk around the yard, with forceful sure movements.

I wonder why it's so out in the open, I say. The Catbird peeks out from the hidden nest and stares squarely at my husband, who walks toward the branch. I tell my husband he is too close.

He doesn't seem to mind me, Sam says. He stands back, hands on his hips.

I think he wants you to protect him, I say.

If one of those Blue Jays wants to raid the nest, that'll be the end of it, my husband says.

I ask him not to say that.

The Catbird watches him intently as Sam backs out of the driveway.

Catbirds live at the edges of a yard or a clearing, in places where they can't be seen, in fencerows, in abandoned farmland.

Our driveway is far from a fencerow.

xi.   March 17, 2022

Photographs of abandoned crops in Ukraine litter the news today, just weeks after this story began. The news says worldwide food shortages will occur. The Russian people must be feeling this shortage, they say, at least. We hope that is the case. Tech workers, educated people, and their families make a quick exodus over the borders to work remotely from anywhere.

A Russian news reporter blurts out on air the truth, then goes into hiding. She is smuggled out of the country, we hear. We hope. Real news makes a quick departure from a country now steeped in RT and Putin-TV. As for the rest, they are being fed only the news they are allowed to consume. Fake news, fake news, fake news. I read somewhere in an article that fake news isn't new. That Andrew Jackson and his followers in the late 1800s began a campaign of chastising "radicals" looking to expand black rights, downplaying news of racial atrocities, accusing them of "making up" the atrocities to further their cause. I wonder how much talk of Nazis taking over Ukraine the Russian people are hearing now. I wonder what of it is believed.

xii.   March 21, 2022

On the porch this morning I tell my husband I think our friend the Catbird has chosen us to spend the springtime with. That his presence means he wants friends, you know? He nods in supposed agreement as I tell him this while he's setting down his muffin and newspaper. He turns to greet his friend who is waiting for him. Peck peck at the dish. Hop hop.

I think he's looking for protection, Sam says under his breath. Good morning little guy, he whispers to the bird. The bird stands, watches Sam, cocks his miniature head this way, that way, cockleshells, then a ripping sound on the lawn. A Robin has landed with his ways his mores his strutting his settling onto the lawn momentarily preoccupy us. A rivet. And then, a baby rabbit suddenly visible hops under the rose bush for cover. The New York Times is covered in mud this morning. The photograph on it is a muck-covered soldier as if war is a new thing because we haven't had one touch us now in so long, or so we like to think, that this muck that was going to stop them is now not stopping the Russians from plundering through like scavengers, as if they hadn't come from the comfort of their mother's bosom and home cooked bliny with butter in their mornings, into this hell.

There must be eggs in the nest, my husband says at last after a few minutes watching the Robin and the baby bunny do their dance. And the Catbird. He is coming around us every morning now. And the sound of the sky crashes into our early morning with wooshes of planes coming in over the airport and freight trucks passing by on the highway just blocks away from our little garden, our rose-filled clover-covered haven with the long porch that awaits us each morning, with its 1894 porch rails, low and wide enough to sit on, that my husband has carefully saved from ruin. There, look, I say, as the Robin puffs up its chest and doubles its size on the front path, puffing his feathers out.

Does he do that to make himself - larger? I ask, pointing at this cockletail show the male Robin puts on for a hidden female watching elsewhere in the yard. Is he doing that for us? My husband shrugs.

Eve, I think it's part of a mating ritual, but I don't see any female Robin, he adds.

Maybe she is watching from a tree, I say. And there, the Robin struts, prancing out his show in the yard filled with life teeming at its edges. I look up on my phone – why does a Robin puff itself up? The answer is interesting – he is either fluffing his down feathers to maintain his body temperature (but it's not chilly this morning) or a male is establishing his territory. I shake my head and show Sam the line about establishing its territory. Our Catbird friend stays close.

And we know, like every morning, that all of this life he will be chased away by the whirr of leaf blowers and the thrum of traffic and people walking past with dogs and children.

A Cardinal is teaching its baby to fly far at the other end of the yard. These helpless creatures begin life with their mouths open, mushy fluff of feathers, sleeping, waiting for food until their parents return. Within a week of birth, they are standing, curious and moving, their fluff sloughing off to real feathers, and in 10 days, their feathers are already turning red. I have been watching them off to the side of the yard for a week now, and suddenly they are fully formed birds. Flying. Trying. Hopping branches. And then the mother has them in the yard, like today. The baby somehow gets down from the nest, risks losing its head to a squirrel a cat a bird a fox who knows. There's a hopping from the slightly reddening baby and a chirping as mother shows baby how to fly-hop. And then, it flies.

It must be baby-hatching time, I whisper. Early this year. It's so early because it's been warm.

The Robin still flits around the bushes. I bet that Robin is going for the Catbird's eggs before they hatch, my husband says. He turns the page on the Times. He is just being realistic, but I don't like it.

Don't say that—that's terrible, I tell him. Robins are nice! They're the first Robins of spring and everything!

Don't be so sure about that, he says. Did you know that the Robin's nest and the Blue Jays' nests are high up in the same tree, and they can see the Catbird's nest? Sam says.

I cannot stand to hear this, so I tell him not to say it. Only the Blue Jays are bad! Robins wouldn't do that, I say.

xiii.   March 22, 2022

Navalny is sentenced to another 9 years in prison and is moved to another jail in Western Russia, the news says today. Putin's opponent who was poisoned, treated in Germany. Who returned to Russia only to be arrested. I wonder why he decided to return. Did he not know who he was dealing with? Did he not know that Putin is in this thing until someone puts a bullet his head? That he is a KGB man? That he is a thug who will not stop and is in this until he is vanished from this earth, that he will do anything: drop a bomb take over countries influence leaders and force a takeover of all of Europe if he can, and then some?

The news generates a few stories about Navalny being moved, maybe in the hopes of calling attention and exposing his movements so that the interloper, the challenger, might not be murdered. Yet. I talk about this mindlessly while my husband reads. I have learned from my years around newsrooms and statement-making, that stories are not ginned up out of nowhere. That stories are put out according to the editor's thoughts on what is right that day. And other times, according to what the government wants to let out into the media on any given day. It is a careful curation, I tell my husband. He nods. He is used to this by now and nods in an encouraging way but tired from hearing it and I understand.

It is another spring morning in our yard, with flowers budding and lawns greening up. The brightness stings my eyes, makes me feel guilty and I flick through the news of Navalny, of the war, of the atrocities on my phone. I don't mention them to him though. The bird pecks around my husband's feet, bored of the jelly on the plate that I've put out each morning for two weeks. Despite the mistake Navalny committed when he said Crimea was a historic part of Russia, which he took back, the west tracks him as if he has the power to make things right.

Thank God we live in a free country, Sam says.

You are only as free as your ability to speak out, I say, and we sit silent.

I think about this fact: You are only as free as your ability to move about wherever you see fit. To make your place where you want. To walk the streets without fear. Without shrapnel, spies, darkness, bombs, missiles hitting houses, apartments, hospitals, killing and disparaging the bodies of teachers, mothers, nurses, babies, uteruses, children, grandmothers. I keep all this in my head, but he can see it on my face. A truck

rambles past, and a small scrap of plastic flies around the yard.
I run to pick it up and the Catbird scatters away.

I need to get to the job site, my husband says and kisses me on
the check. I am holding the scrap of plastic in my hand; it is a
piece of plastic from a pack of candy. I wonder where it came
from since we don't usually eat candy. My husband backs the
car down the driveway, stops where I stand on the lawn to say
goodbye. Me, in my crocs, in my sweatpants, messy hair in a
bun on the top of my head.

I love you, I say, and he says back. I watch him back the black
Camaro out of the driveway, top down on this glorious spring
day.

xiv.   **March 24, 2022**

Breathing. Breathless. Suffocation. A downpour that fills the air with too much moisture. I need fresh air. There is a dew on the grass and it is warm. I take a walk and it is Thursday morning. As I pass under the branch in the driveway near the nest, I hear the cheeps of baby birds. I look at the nest, being careful not to get too close, and I can see little beak mouths. Tendrils of beings sitting together, three of them. I don't want to disturb the little family.

The babies hatched; I text my husband. He texts back a heart.

My sweet husband. I picture Sam at the job site, lording over people who don't appreciate him as he cleans up an oil tank-strewn lot to make way for a hydropower plant.

I walk with my headphones down the safe, slate sidewalks of my archetypal town, past restored Victorians with cherry blossom buds. Lawns are manicured weekly. Trees are neatly trimmed. Gardens carefully weeded. This looks like the scene from some quintessentially American town, and it is, in fact. Dotted with people commuting to the city, striving. Or a horror film. Stepford gone all wrong. I shake the thought from my brain. Stare at a daffodil. Refocus, refocus. Stop thinking this way.

But as I walk, I can't help but think of my grandfather. Of the brothers and sisters who stayed in Ukraine that we never met. I think of an uncle who fought in the trenches of the First World War. And of my grandfather, who pushed back the front lines of the Second World War.

This is the Third World War is what I think and what no one wants me to say.

xv.   **March 25, 2022**

Are we free or are we slaves? That is the question at stake in any war. Wars in this era seem to have a dual purpose. Diversion. I obsess on this all day as I try to do my work and put blinders on. I can't put blinders on the truth. This is a war to make the US look bad, to make Biden and democracy look like failures, I tell my husband when he gets home.

Sam shakes his head, laughs, says I watch too much news. He flicks a bug off his leg as he walks in from his car. It is 6 pm and I don't ask him how he is. News has been my business - - so I read everything, I say, and he shrugs. The news on my phone, the New York Times, the Post, Opinion pages, The Hill, The Times of India. This is a Third World War, I say and he kisses my cheek.

I see the signs. I read between the lines, I say. Then I stop because I can see he's tired.

Yet there you have it. What happens in war?

Gas prices hike. Food hikes. Eggs go up.

Supply chains stall.

Inflation sets in. Inflation, Inflation. "It's all Democracy's fault."

Messaging from Putin-friendly right-wing channels turns away from sympathizing with the enemy now that the pandering is too dangerous to continue. Now that the news of raping babies, raping land, pillaging houses, beating mothers and grandmothers, decapitations, throwing prisoners into crowded basements where there is no room to sit or lie down. Where 200 people in a dark basement can only stand. For hours. Days. Nights. Weeks. Where they are not fed. Where they watch one another drop one by one. Where the group collectively breathes up all the air in the basement. And then all of them are dead.

The right-wing media has a new chant across the Internet, across red television, radio, from conservative pundits. Everything is our current President's fault. If only "we" were in power, this wouldn't happen. If only the man who wanted to fist-bump Putin were in power, then this would stop. The man who idolizes Hitler. If only, if only, if only.

Fiona Hill says billionaires and millionaire media magnates are Putin's mouthpieces. She says Putin's Russia is sending his proxy message through them. Yet no one can hear what's really going on. They keep predicting a quick end to this – this war – as if it's not been ignited by a madman. As if it's not been ignited by a man who is in it to win it or die.

Win it or die. He will not retreat.

Putin will not retreat. Napoleon chose war over retreat. Ramses, Alexander, Genghis Khan, Tamerlane, Adolph Hitler. Refused to retreat. I can feel the smoke rising in my chest, in my cough, the humidity in the air. I look up.

I rub my eyes. I hear a ping from the timer. Dinner is ready. Chicken pot pie from a local farm. There is a thumbtack on the living room floor, but I don't pick it up. I drag myself past it.

I don't want to cook. I don't want to do dishes. I don't want to eat. I don't feel as if I deserve to eat. None of us do. In our plush democracy. In our supposed safety where we can get shot by some rogue kid or rabid man gone mad (but still has a gun). In the news, a man was found in full military gear with weaponry and ammunition at a theme park, who'd committed suicide. My guess is he chickened out before he started.

Out the back door I see an orange cat saunter through the yard. I wonder about the hedgehog who lives under the porch. I wonder about the nest. About the Blue Jays. I look out at the branch over the driveway. There's a breeze blowing in, leaves swaying in the trees, something that happens when the wind comes in across the plains. I wonder if I should move the plastic chairs under the porch, but I decide not to. I don't have the energy.

I look at the greying sky. I don't feel safe. None of us are safe. None of us.

Stop reading the news, my husband tells me, and I know he is right, when I return with plates. The game is on. How are the Red Sox doing? I ask. Not that great, Sam says, switching to the Yankees. We have a lot of teams to root for.

Can we watch a movie? I ask. I think about Navalny. I think about being free. Am I free?

Sam falls asleep early, and I fall into scrolling, reading, gasping, heart-rolling. Researching.

I learn that a year before Russia took Crimea, the pro-Russian regime in Ukraine rejected a deal in Kiev for greater economic integration with the European Union. Protests against this pro-Russian regime were met with violent crackdowns. That's when the leader fled the country and Zelensky was voted in.

Zelensky who said I need aid, and I don't need a ride out.

How free is Zelensky?

xvi.   March 26, 2022

My husband checks the branch for the next few days and the babies are still there.

In the news, there are rumblings about the Dobbs decision. About the possibility of pulling Roe vs Wade. For the taking away of the rights that we as women have had all of our lives, and now our daughters' risk dark alleys and coat hangers. I think of my great-grandmother who died "of childbirth," except no baby was born. Right-wing men trying to control our bodies, I tell my husband. He says he can't believe it will really happen.

I think of the war between control and power.

I think of my mother's friends with eight children, women with postpartum depression who dared not speak, D&C's done at the local hospital until the doctor got found out and resigned. Another dirty battle. They are coming for our birth control.

In the news, women march around the US capitol with bonnets and capes in the colors of the Handmaid's Tale as the

Supreme Court mulls Dobs and the "decision" to rescind Roe.

 All the acts of this war and this world are connected, I say to my husband, and he shakes his head. He knows I am compelled to read the news and he is trying to reason me of my obsession, but this is a futile act.

This is a Third World War going on right here. Everywhere, I say. Left versus right.

White male power – right-wing power – oligarchs versus everyone else.

He sips his coffee, kisses the top of my head, and walks away gingerly, saying he needs to get to work upstairs. I stare at the red slate kitchen floor. I see blood.

xvii. **March 27, 2022**

We are ground Zero in this town. Thirty people from our village perished in 911. The memorial we pass by every day. At first it made us all more determined than ever to live our lives in freedom. The day there was a perfect blue sky.

Ground Zero again when one hundred fifty perished in the pandemic that was called a deep fake by the right. We lost friends and family.

Because we are Ground Zero, our plan is to head to the mountains in the event of a nuclear explosion.

If we make it out alive.

We like to think that we would.

My husband checks the nest at lunchtime.

No one has gotten them yet, he likes to say.

I hate when he does that - he says he likes to be realistic.

Bodies are shown on the news in bags, lying in the streets.

Women, children.

A pregnant woman with long hair like mine is evacuated from a maternity hospital with a large baby belly and a deep wound in her side. Wearing fluffy patterned pajamas, the spoils of a prosperous Western society on her back. She is alert. There is blood and dirt in her hair and is a gash in her side. But she is alive though, the news touts. Thank God. Thank God. Thank God.

A sallow victory.

Neither she nor the baby make it.

More reports of mothers with babies inside of them dying.

And I say to anyone who will listen, Putin does not care. He will not stop this war; he wants a scorched earth. He will not give up this war until he is dead. My husband worries about my preoccupation. It is a truth that becomes more poignant to me, day by day.

My friends tire of hearing it, and so does my husband.

I cannot say this enough, I tell them.

I read things. I see things. I predicted things that happened. I connect dots....

Things you don't have on your radar.

54

Head shakes. Eye rolls. Avoidance. Let's talk about the weather, they say. I try to tell them why we need to be concerned. Why we need to see the dots spelled out on my map. The impeachment, the call to Zelensky, the…whatever. Whatever whatever whatever. My tongue gets sticky in my mouth. I can't say it all in one connected sentence.

It is a complex web. I am Carrie from Homeland, plotting lines on a map of the world.

xviii. March 28, 2022

I cannot bear to see the bodies of men and women, the covered faces of dead children. I cannot bear to watch escape buses being blown to pieces. Being shot at from a distance.

I begin to simply wait for my husband to awaken in the early morning hours while I write. I skip the television and I leave my phone inside. There has to be peace somewhere. I sit on the porch. I put on my Crocs and walk the early spring garden, snipping old rose branches, dead buds. I spray for insects. The bright purple of the hyacinth is peeping up from the earth. That undulating circle blue, color of the Gods, color of the sky. Color of the clear, safe sky. The sky my grandfather risked his life to protect. To make sure I could be safe.

My guilt is pure, and it is survivor-driven.

I think of the faces of the Ukrainian women on the news who look like me.

Hair awry, blood on their faces, clothing askew.

Looking for their children.

Are they cousins?

xix.   March 29. 2022

One morning the Internet goes out and television skitters, and my heart scatters for a minute. I go to Putin. I ruminate – Putin has done this.

He is going to get us from the inside. He is going to shut down our plants and interfere with daily life.

There are moles here; I have met some working in the news. Traveling, working on interviews for Russian television, they say. People I consider reporting to the FBI.

I don't want the FBI in my house though, scaring my family. I've been trained by Homeland Security. I carry a tourniquet and a bulletproof vest in my trunk. I carry a first aid kit fit for a medic. I wear a bulletproof vest on my way to work some days.

I am fortunate not to have ever tested that vest.

The Internet fritters back on. Pops back into place. I put on my dress shoes, head out for a meeting. I look up at the branch but can't see the nest. I'm not tall enough.

xx.　　**March 30, 2022**

I am at a meeting in the city. A client. A plan. A small crisis. Shrapnel falling, in its own way. When I get home, I call my husband down from his office on the third floor.

Are the birds still there?

They are, he says. They're getting big. Almost ready to fly. Preparing to be out on their own, I think. Preparing to launch, in a way. I kiss him.

I have to hop onto a Zoom call, I say. He smiles, and I leave him eating a sandwich in a strip of sunlight beaming into our kitchen full of windows. A kitchen my husband rebuilt with his own hands. So that we could enjoy that light filtering in.

As I listen on the call, I can't help but do research. How many Catbirds are there?

Six hundred twenty thousand individuals make up the Catbird population in my state. I think of the 43 million people in Ukraine, wonder how many got out. How many are there? How many are fleeing for their lives this very moment.

I brush that out of my mind, try to concentrate. There is an unwrapped binky lollypop on my desk. A CBD one.

I say what I must say as part of the PowerPoint, then hit mute again. I smile pleasantly into the camera.

The Catbird is dark grey with a dusky tuft atop his head with a wedge-shaped tail. The bird is named because it sounds like a cat. Meew, meew. The breeding grounds for Catbirds encompass the northeast and into North Carolina, a land mass twice the size of Ukraine. I cannot imagine having enemy soldiers so close to us. From here to there.

Perhaps this should enter our consciousness.

An awareness erased after the World Wars, when the lights went out in the coastal cities after 9 p.m. so we wouldn't be targets. Sitting Catbirds in a tree full of Robins and Blue Jays.

We no longer have atomic drills sitting under desks.

We no longer turn the lights out on the coast at night.

But we now prepare our children for a shootout.

I wanted to think that Robins were good and Blue Jays were bad. But as I sit there doing my research, pretending to listen to my call, I finally dare to look it up.

Sadly, I confirm what Sam has been trying to tell me: that Robins steal Catbird eggs and eat babies to protect their territory. Sam is an astute man – he is hardly ever wrong. So there.

Robins are not the good guys.

xxi.   April 1, 2022

Let me put it to you this way – I know more than the newscasters know. I can't help but know it. It's my business. I hate to tell this to anyone. I don't think anyone I know can stomach this.

But this is not going to be a short war. This is going to be a third world war. And we will get into it. We are already into it. We just don't want to admit it yet.

We don't want to see it.

We are on a precipice.

We are at the crevice of a gully.

We are at a high peak, paved with ice all the way down.

We are at the top of the Empire State Building.

With no safe net to jump to.

And in the lofty way that writers like to liken this to conflicts, I see this as a never-ending war. I have researched Putin. I have written briefs about his people. I have studied him. I know what he did once the wall came down. This man wants his wall back up. And more.

In the news this day, 100,000 residents are trapped near Mariupol.

Troop blockades will not let escape busses pass.

News stories of Russian troops walking into houses, defiling teens.

An 87-year-old grandmother says she wishes they killed her instead.

Babies shot, defiled, tortured.

The Russians blame the Chechen soldiers.

Drunken rage-eyed troops ransack houses, steal clothing, wear women's coats out of their houses and set them aflame right outside.

Pilfering every bit of food from cupboards. Raping.

Emptying pantries. Leaving families with nothing.

Shattering doors and windows in their wake. Raping.

Wearing fur coats from ransacked closets to keep warm. Raping.

And then there are stories of heroes.

Stories that Ukrainian soldiers will not give up or give in.

I sit on the porch, needing to take a breath.

It's misty out this morning, April Fool's Day.

I am fortunate to live here, with my little front porch, buds ready to bloom around me. The Magnolia tree in the yard sprouts tiny pink and white buds. Bunnies that dart around the yard. The newspaper man chucks the paper from the car. I look up and wave, but he's driven past. He's got a job to do. I walk down the brick path to get the paper, and of course, I open it up. These days, there is no escaping the news.

I wonder where the Catbird is. Have his babies begun to fly?

xxii.   April 5, 2022

The grass in the yard is greening up now. A flash frost comes in to kill the buds on the Magnolia tree. I look out to the backyard that morning to find a mass murder of blackened buds.

Disheartening. Heavy hearted. Shod-footed, I turn to get my coffee. We've never had a spring without the Magnolia. Not in recent memory. The Magnolia is our guidepost of light, of the renewal of spring, of the warmth to come, but this massacre is little to complain about.

When my husband comes down, I point the tree out. He's saddened, too. And just like him, he shrugs it off. They'll be back next year, he says in his realist way.

This is nothing compared to what other people are feeling today. I know that.

But I can't shake the feeling of ruin.

I think about the dead relatives of my grandparents, people I never met.

I've seen photographs of them, strangers that share my blood,
lying face down on the ground in the 1940s.

And I see them now.

xxiii. April 15, 2022

The grey Catbird does not fly across the ocean. It does not live in Europe or Ukraine or even Russia. The bird is a perching bird, probably a relative of the Caribbean Thrasher so says Google. How can I think about researching a bird? Really, I say to myself, but I keep reading.

Ukraine's special bird is the White Stork – the country's symbol of hope. Eastern Europe is a stronghold for the white stork. Poland, Belarus, Lithuania, Latvia, Sweden, Ukraine.

In folklore, the Stork stands for peace.

In fact, I read, the White Stork is an international sign of peace.

I sit, drinking my coffee. Thinking of Zelensky. His wife. I wonder where his children are.

I sit, ignoring the newspaper, watching a man whose poodle silently pees on the strip of grass between my sidewalk and the road.

I sit, feeling as if I don't want to know any news today.

My husband rushes to the porch to tell me.

I checked the branch out back, he says. The Catbird has left its nest.

The babies must be ready to go on their own, I chirp, trying to be optimistic.

He shakes his head. No, honey - - they were too small yet to fly last time I looked.

My sweet husband and his Catbird friend, I say as I look up at the sky. Our uninterrupted peace is still sunny in the mornings. The unbroken indigo of promise. The false color of safety.

He's long gone now, my husband says, as we watch a Robin puff itself on the path.

xxiv. April 20, 2022

On the news this day: a five-year-old boy cries in the living room while the soldiers rape his mother in the bedroom, as he hears her screams.

He will never be the same for hearing this.

She will never be the same for living this.

We will never be the same for knowing this.

I feel the shrapnel falling in the blue skies over my quiet garden.

I see Zelensky's face, I see Navalny's steel blue eyes, kind faces when I close my eyes. Two people in whose hands Democracy seems to rest.

And yet it rests in the hands of all of us.

This is World War Three, I tell my husband later as we sit on the porch. We sit in silence, and I watch a bumblebee hover near the rose buds. I take a breath out. My husband breaths in.

I guarantee we have air force flying above us – we're so close to the city, he says.

I look up and there is a cumulus puff in the shape of a white bird - floating.

I wonder if any of us can know what goes on above the clouds.

Epilogue – December 2023 – February 2024

December 2023

On the news this day Putin's opposition leader, lawyer, anti-corruption activist Alexi Anatolyevich Navalny is not accounted for.

For six days his lawyers wait for permission to see him.

Only to be turned away at the last minute.

Letters not being delivered to him.

He doesn't appear in a court video link.

They say they were having "electricity problems."

By Friday, his absence is concerning, given his recent "illness."

And finally, they let everyone know - why.

He felt dizzy. Lay down on the floor. Prison officials unfolded the bed.

He was given an IV. "We don't know what caused it."

Navalny was being deprived of food.

Navalny's cell had no ventilation.

Navalny was allowed minimal outdoor time.

Navalny fainted out of hunger.

His lawyer said he looked "more or less fine."

He was due to be transferred to a "special prison."

The Polar Wolf Penal Colony.

Living among the most dangerous repeat offenders.

February 15, 2024 – February 16, 2024

Navalny appears on video at a court hearing. He makes jokes, appears in good health. And then silence.

He was in solitary confinement for the 27th time.

He may have been taking a walk or so they say.

He may have been part of a prisoner exchange.

He may have been a write-in winner of the next election.

Navalny lost consciousness after a walk.

An ambulance arrived in less than seven minutes.

They performed resuscitation measures for half an hour.

He could not be revived. He may have been on the verge of release.

Only to be turned away at the last minute.

Alexei Navalny was reported dead at 16:19 Yekaterina time on February 16, 2024.

Murdered. By. Putin. Russians are dropping dead around the world.

This is a message.

No one in Russia is free. No Russian is free. In Putin's world, no one is free.

What is it about February?

The timing is tidy – consider history for reference.

February 9, 1946 – Joseph Stalin's speech declared a de facto beginning of World War III with the West. February 24, 1946 – The United States responded with the "Long Telegram," calling out the intentions of the Soviet leadership as exploiting Marxist ideology to characterize the outside world as hostile and to justify their hold on power despite falling public support.

February 22, 2014 – The collapse of the power-sharing agreement in Crimea.

Late February 2014 – Russian military officials take control of Crimea.

February 24, 2022 – Russian tanks roll into Ukraine.

February 16, 2024 – Alexei Navalny is dead.

February 24, 2024 – Republicans continue to block aid to Ukraine.

Trump says he's "like Navalny," seeking a regime change. Trump says the opposite of what is.

But this time, he is telling us who he is. "Seeking a regime change."

Open your eyes America.

Open your ears America.

Open. Your. Eyes.

Read the Long Telegram. The playbook.

We are pushing at the outer edge of Democracy.

February 29, 2024 – Leap Year

I look up and there is a cumulus cloud in the shape of a white bird - floating.

In my head, I hear the voices of victims, screaming, starving, fighting. Attacks from all sides.

 I connect the dots, but no one wants to talk about it.

Fresh wars that serve as newly crafted distractions.

And yet I hear the sounds of spring singing in my yard.

I hear the meews of Catbirds settling back into the trees.

I look up and there is a silvery cloud looming above me.

I hope that what I see is the great white bird rising.

"The only tyrant I will accept in this world is the still voice within."

– Mahatma Gandhi

Notes

Catbird, while inspired by true events, unfolds as a fictional narrative against the backdrop of Russia's invasion of Ukraine. Reflecting on global conflicts and human resilience, Julia underscores the universal relevance of her story, offering a poignant message of hope and solidarity in tumultuous times worldwide.

About the Author

Julia Marie Davis is an American poet and novelist. A lifelong affinity for birds and wildlife instilled by her mother, a former college professor of botany, imbues Julia's work with a unique perspective. Her cherished memories awakening to the melodious calls of a mourning dove and nurturing two beloved parakeets, Harry and Baby Louise, underscore her connection to the natural world. Her earliest memories of nature are infused with bird calls, bird watching and in her last year of elementary school, she wrote her "hero paper" on John J. Audubon.

Julia's writing has appeared in *The Bangalore Review, The Dillydoun Review, New Note Poetry*, The Moonstone Arts Center's *Nasty Women's Anthology* and *TaintTaintTaint Literary Magazine*. She shares her insights through a biweekly column on Medium. Her professional background in public relations, coupled with her training in crisis management from the Department of Homeland Security through Texas A&M University, infuse her storytelling with depth and authenticity. Julia holds a BA in English from Boston College and a Masters of Fine Art in Creative Writing from Fairfield University. While at Fairfield, she served as an assistant editor at *BREVITY* and as a reader for *WOODHALL PRESS*.

About the Press

Middle Creek Publishing & Audio believes that responding to the world through art & literature—and sharing that response—is a vital part of being an artist.

Middle Creek Publishing & Audiois a company seeking to make the world a better place through both the means and ends of publishing. We are publishers of quality literature in any genre from authors and artists, both seasoned and those who are undiscovered or under-valued, or under-represented, with a great interest in works which illuminate or embody any aspect of contemplative Human Ecology, defined as the relationship between humans and their natural, social, and built environments.

Middle Creek Publishing & Audio's particular interest in Human Ecology is meant to clarify an aspect of the quality in the works we will consider for publication and as a guide to those considering submitting work to us. Our interest is in publishing works which illuminate the human experience through words, story or other content that connects us to each other, our environment, our history, and our potential deeply and more consciously.

In 2024, we are transitioning to Middle Creek Press, an NTEE A33: Arts, Culture, and Humanities - Printing and Publishing nonprofit organization. This change will empower us to focus more on the quality of our work and extend our literary reach. Be part of this transformative journey by supporting our fundraising efforts. If you have a moment, fill out the questionnaire on the following page or drop us a line at editor@middlecreekpublishing.com to give us feedback on our impact that we can use in grants reporting.

HELP US WITH GRANTS REPORTING

If you have a moment, fill out this questionnaire on the following page, cut it out and mail it to:

Middle Creek Pres
9161 Pueblo Mountain Park Road
Beulah, CO 81023

Or save postage and instead, and email us at editor@middlecreekpublishing.com to give us feedback on our impact that we can use in grants reporting.

Check all that apply

[] I enjoy Middle Creek Press's quality products.

[] Middle Creek Press' titles have helped me connect to the natural world.

[]. Middle Creek Press' titles have helped me connect to my interiority, and its connection to the world.

[]. Middle Creek Press' titles have helped me connect to my natural environment.

[]. Middle Creek Press' titles have mirrored my own feelings, or have helped me find my words to myself, other people, and the world we share.

[] Middle Creek Press' titles have helped me connect to my interiority, and it's connection to the world.

[]. Middle Creek Press' is one of my favorite literary presses.

[] Middle Creek Press have helped me find hope in the power of community voices address our collective societal issues.

Made in United States
North Haven, CT
01 November 2024

59725275R00049